The One That Makes Me Yawn

Story by Gina Kegel
Illustrations by James Rhodimer

To my
two sweet little dreamers

It was just about bedtime,
The sun low and red,

A sleepy young boy
Slipped snug into bed

Ready for rest
All snuggled down deep,
The sweet little dreamer stretched,
And yawned,
And went

Right...
To...
Cough!

The yawn that was brewing
Deep down in his tummy
Popped out his throat —
It felt kinda funny.

Caught on a breeze
Swept over the sash
It found itself far away in a dash!

"This is my chance!
Before the sun dawns,
I'll see what's around me,
And see what's beyond!"

Putting on steam,
Beginning to zip,

The yawn set right out
On his first ever trip.

An indigo sky
Stretched overhead

As creatures below
Settled down for bed.

Two chicks in their nest
Refused to sleep.
They flapped, they squirmed,
They jostled, they cheeped.

But as the yawn flew
Sparkling by,

They stretched,
And yawned,
And went right...
to....
sleep.

A bear cub and mama
Were snug in the zoo
With only eating and
Playing to do.

The cub wanted more,
"Play, mama, play!"
But mama had had
Enough for the day.

Her big furry arm
Pulled him in deep
Holding him close
With a warm brown sweep.

And as the yawn flew
Sparkling by,
They stretched,
And yawned,

And went right...
to....
sleep.

A goat and a kitten,
Unlikely best friends
Chased round the yard,
Leapt end over end.

"Settle down out there!"
The other goats cried.
But there was too much fun
To be had outside.

A duck waddled out
And quacked rather deep,

"Lay DOWN, you too!
Not another peep!"

But as the yawn flew
Sparkling by,
They stretched,
And yawned,
And went right...

       to....

          sleep.

On it zoomed
Through the night
But thoughts of the dreamer
Crept into its flight.

"Without a yawn,
Even snuggled down deep,
I wonder if my boy
Is having trouble with sleep?"

Without a yawn
To help him calm
His thoughts danced like ditties,

He counted sheep,
He counted cubs,
He counted goats and kitties.

But as the yawn flew gently in,
His eyes grew soft and dim.

And finally, with relief,
He stretched,
And yawned,
And went
    right...
        to....

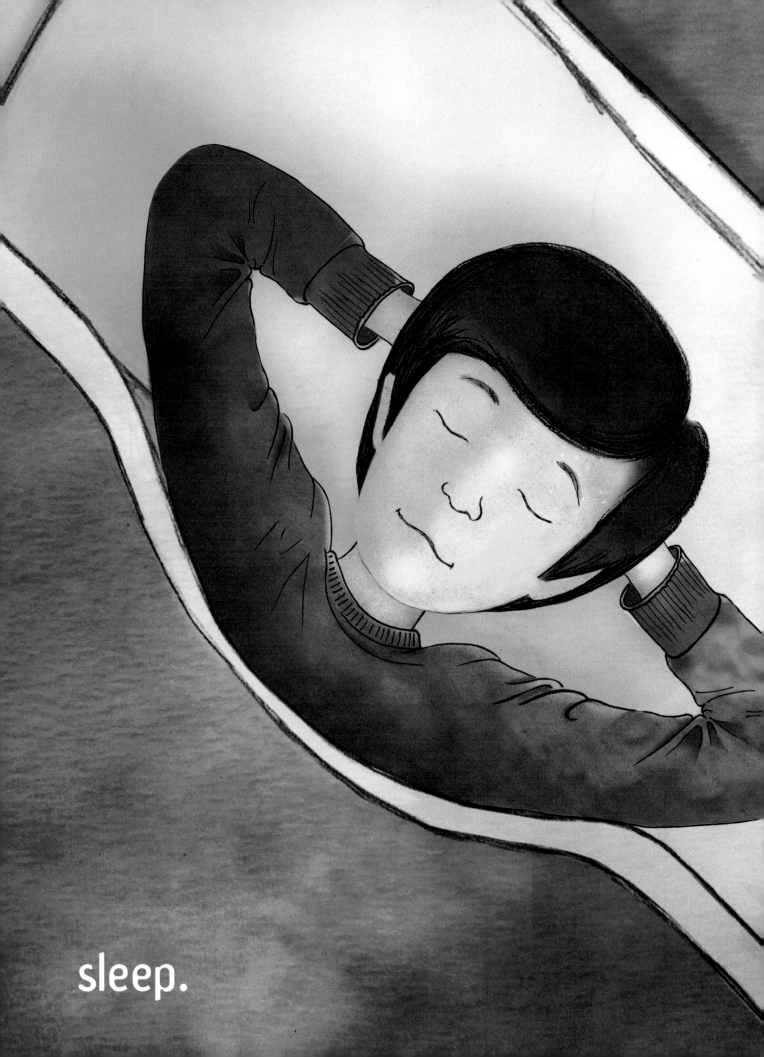

sleep.

ABOUT THE AUTHOR

Gina Kegel is a freelance copywriter in Southern California through her business Gina is Write. She is the Senior Columnist at the Los Angeles Tribune, with a weekly column titled The Journey-Centered Life, and Associate Editor at Radiance Multidimensional Media.

As a Wayshower, Gina works with individuals and small groups through Free to Flourish Energy Healing. Utilizing a combination of intuitive and Akashic Records reading, energy healing, and mediumship, Gina guides clients to understand their personal truths and soul path, supercharging the healing and empowerment process through released blocks and ongoing guidance.

Gina serves as the Director of Community Outreach and Fundraising for the Huntington Beach Chapter of the Holistic Chamber of Commerce, and is a Volunteer Educator with BabywearingOC. Gina lives with her husband and two sons, and holds a Bachelor of Music in Music Education from the University of the Pacific Conservatory of Music.

Learn more at: ginakegel.com and ginaiswrite.com

Instagram: @ginakegelauthor

Facebook: Gina is Write and Gina Kegel Author

ABOUT THE ILLUSTRATOR

James Rhodimer is a Southern California-based illustration artist, sculptor, filmmaker, and photographer. His short and feature films, cubist and character paintings and avant garde art photography have been exhibited in festivals, galleries and museums in Los Angeles, Salt Lake City and Springville, Utah.

Find him at: brashstudios.com
Instagram: @Brashsketch

Made in the USA
San Bernardino, CA
05 June 2020